Dear Parent:
Your child's love of reading starts here!

Every child learns to read in a different way and at his or her own speed. Some go back and forth between reading levels and read favorite books again and again. Others read through each level in order. You can help your young reader improve and become more confident by encouraging his or her own interests and abilities. From books your child reads with you to the first books he or she reads alone, there are I Can Read Books for every stage of reading:

SHARED READING
Basic language, word repetition, and whimsical illustrations, ideal for sharing with your emergent reader

BEGINNING READING
Short sentences, familiar words, and simple concepts for children eager to read on their own

READING WITH HELP
Engaging stories, longer sentences, and language play for developing readers

READING ALONE
Complex plots, challenging vocabulary, and high-interest topics for the independent reader

ADVANCED READING
Short paragraphs, chapters, and exciting themes for the perfect bridge to chapter books

I Can Read Books have introduced children to the joy of reading since 1957. Featuring award-winning authors and illustrators and a fabulous cast of beloved characters, I Can Read Books set the standard for beginning readers.

A lifetime of discovery begins with the magical words **"I Can Read!"**

Visit www.icanread.com for information
on enriching your child's reading experience.

To Cristiano Cora,
a maestro with scissors
—J.O'C.

For Cari, whose hair is
simply one *of her many*
fabulous assets!
—R.P.G.

To Mr. C.—my
first official small-town
barber in the big city
—T.E.

I Can Read Book® is a trademark of HarperCollins Publishers.

Fancy Nancy: Hair Dos and Hair Don'ts   Text copyright © 2011 by Jane O'Connor   Illustrations copyright © 2011 by Robin Preiss Glasser   All rights reserved. Printed in the United States of America. No part of this book may be used or reproduced in any manner whatsoever without written permission except in the case of brief quotations embodied in critical articles and reviews. For information address HarperCollins Children's Books, a division of HarperCollins Publishers, 10 East 53rd Street, New York, NY 10022. www.icanread.com

Library of Congress Cataloging-in-Publication Data is available.
ISBN 978-0-06-200180-1 (trade bdg.) — ISBN 978-0-06-200179-5 (pbk.)

12 13 14 15   LP/WOR   10 9 8 7 6 5 4 3   ❖   First Edition

I Can Read!

BEGINNING READING **1**

Fancy NANCY

Hair Dos and Hair Don'ts

by Jane O'Connor

cover illustration by Robin Preiss Glasser

interior illustrations by Ted Enik

HARPER

An Imprint of HarperCollinsPublishers

"Do not forget.

Tomorrow is Picture Day,"

Ms. Glass reminds us.

(Reminding is fancy

for making us remember something.)

"I also have a surprise."

"Ooh! Ooh!

What is it?" asks Clara.

"If I told you,

it wouldn't be a surprise,"

says Ms. Glass.

"You will find out tomorrow."

"Good-bye," I say to Ms. Glass.

She didn't need to remind me

about Picture Day.

It is just about the most important

day of the school year.

Weeks ago

I put a circle around the day

on my calendar.

Weeks ago

I picked out my outfit.

(Outfit is fancy for clothes.)

I will wear

my pink shirt with ruffles,

my purple skirt with ruffles, my

pink-and-purple socks with ruffles.

Ruffles make anything fancy!

After dinner, I read my library book.

It is about Amelia Earhart.

She was a brave airplane pilot.

Amelia was not fancy.

But I like how she looks,

her hair most of all.

Her hairstyle is called a bob.

Then it hits me.

I have not decided on my hairstyle

for Picture Day.

My hair is curly,

so I can wear it

in many flattering ways.

(Flattering is fancy for pretty.)

Maybe I will wear my hair in pigtails.

Maybe I will wear my hair in a bun.

Maybe I will wear my hair long
and loose.

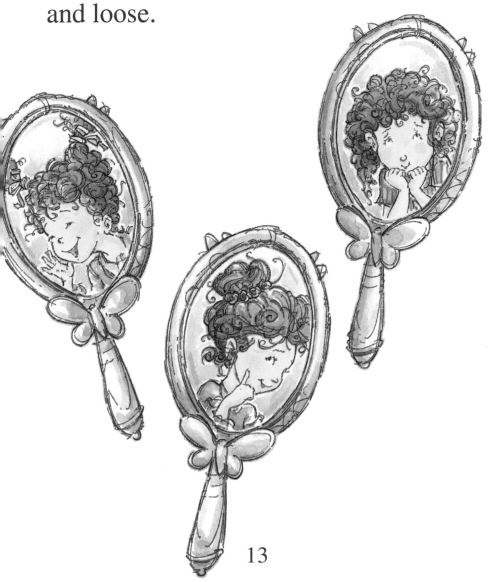

Just then Bree calls.

She describes

her outfit for Picture Day.

(Describe means to tell about.)

Then she says,

"My mom braided my hair

and put in new beads."

"Oh, how elegant," I tell her.

(Elegant is fancy for fancy.)

Maybe I will wear cornrows like Bree.

But Mom does not have time
to make lots of braids.
And Dad is not a good braider.

Later I read more of my book.

Then it hits me.

I will wear my hair like Amelia.

Ooh la la!

That will be perfect for Picture Day.

Amelia's hair was shorter than mine.

But I can trim my hair.

I snip a little here.

I snip a little there.

I snip in the back.

And I snip in the front for bangs.

My bangs are crooked.

So I snip some more.

Trimming hair

is very complicated!

(Complicated is the opposite of easy.)

I am still snipping

when Mom comes into my room.

"Nancy! What are you doing?

Scissors are only for cutting paper.

That is a Clancy family rule."

"I'm sorry.

Really I am.

I just wanted my hair to look perfect

for Picture Day," I say.

But it looks horrible!

Mom tries her best to help.

"There. Your hair looks fine."

She is trying to comfort me.

(That's fancy for making me feel better.)

"I can't go to school tomorrow.
I can't be in the picture," I say.
But Mom says,
"You are not missing school
because of your hair."

The next morning,

I come into class.

I am wearing my fancy outfit.

I have tied a scarf around my head.

It does not look fancy.

It looks odd—

which is fancy for strange.

25

Soon it is time for the picture.

Lionel and Bree are next to me.

I wish I were invisible.

Ms. Glass says,

"You all look wonderful.

Now I will show you the surprise."

She has caps for us.

The caps say "Ms. Glass's Stars."

"Do you want to wear the caps

for the picture?" Ms. Glass asks.

"Yes!" we shout.

(I shout louder than anybody.)

P.S. I hope I have
fast-growing hair!

31

Fancy Nancy's Fancy Words

These are the fancy words in this book:

Comfort—make someone feel better

Complicated—the opposite of easy

Describe—tell about

Elegant—fancy

Flattering—pretty

Moment—right now

Odd—strange

Outfit—clothes

Remind—make us remember something

Quickly I unwrap my scarf.

I put on the cap.

I do not look odd anymore.

I look almost normal!

One, two, three.

We all say, "Cheese!"

And for the moment—

that's fancy for right now—

I look picture-perfect!

30